The

Vacation

by the

Beach

TAYLYN SENEC

Vacation by the Beach by Taylyn Senec. Book #2 in the Miller Kids Series. Published by Taylyn Senec. Edited by Nadara Merrill.

www.facebook.com/taylynsenec

Paperback ISBN: 978-1-7334109-6-0

Chapter 1

"The car is leaving in ten minutes. If you're not ready, you're not coming," Mom yelled up the stairs to Parker and Emma.

"DAD!" Shouted Emma. "Can you help me with my suitcase? Please!"

Dad came out of his bedroom with a big backpack on and scooped up Emma's suitcase before heading down to the car. Dad had been gone for a year with the military, and everyone was excited to finally have a family vacation together.

Emma bounced down the stairs behind him with Mr. Woofers, her stuffed dog, dangling out of her backpack.

"Don't leave without me!" Parker huffed under his breath as he pulled his bag out to the driveway.

"Who is riding with me and who is riding with Dad?" asked Mom from the front steps.

"DAD!" both kids exclaimed at the same time.

"You can take Hunter with you, Mom," giggled Emma and pet their big German Shepherd as he trotted up beside her.

Dad laughed and said, "Mom can't be that bad guys... How about Emma rides with her to Cape Cod and then we switch for the ride home?" He shot both the kids a quick look to let them know they hurt Mom's feelings.

"Okay." Emma said with a smile. "I think we could use some girl time anyways!"

"Isn't all the shopping you do in Mashpee enough girl time?" Parker huffed. "I don't understand why you both love that place so much."

"The cupcakes!" Mom and Emma chimed at the same time and burst out with laughter. "And the little bookstore with the fountain out front," added Mom.

Dad locked the front door. "Hope everyone has everything!" He tapped his hand on the hood of the truck. "We better get going if we are going to beat Boston traffic."

Mom loaded Hunter into the backseat of the car. "At least the Cape is so much closer to this house than our last one. I wonder who will get there first?"

"Is that a challenge?" Parker exclaimed. He hopped in the truck as Mom nodded. "Then challenge accepted!"

Chapter 2

Country music was blasting on the radio as Mom and Emma approached the Bourne Bridge. They had only hit a few spots of traffic on the drive down and were enjoying a much-needed jam session.

"We're almost there, we're almost there!" exclaimed Emma. Mom and Dad had been visiting Cape Cod since before Emma and Parker were born. Mom and Dad honeymooned in Wellfleet and had found a little vacation rental in a village not far from the Cape Cod Canal. The house was yellow with blue flower boxes, and the beach was only a few steps away. Within a quick walk, there was the best little bakery, an ice cream shop, a pizza place and the best seafood they had ever eaten.

Parker, Emma, and Hunter also loved all the nature trails and exploring all the woods nearby. Time seemed to stand still when they were on the Cape. No one would talk about the military or school tests or making sports teams. It was all fun, all relaxation, and all family.

"I am so excited to get my feet in the water." Mom said with a smile.

"And I am so excited to swim to the dock this year," Emma said while winking. Last year, the lifeguards wouldn't let her because she needed a kickboard. This year she was ready, though.

"Should I call Dad to see where they are?" Mom asked while glancing at the clock.

Emma shook her head. "No way, it is so much better when they don't know we're winning!"

Chapter 3

"Do you really think Emma hasn't

figured out that we stop every year on the

way down?" Parker asked as they got out of

the truck.

Dad nodded. "Let her think she wins, it keeps her happy and keeps us from having to unpack."

They walked down to the canal. "It's nice out today." Parker smelled the salt air.

"Yes, it is. Think you want to try fishing on the canal again this year?" Dad nudged Parker in the side.

Last year, Parker had tried fishing for the first time. Before he even had a chance to cast the pole, he had slipped on the slippery rocks and twisted his ankle. For

months, Emma wouldn't let it go that they

wasted a day at the hospital.

"Yeah, but I am staying on dry land."

Parker laughed. "I think some high tide

fishing would be a good idea."

"Sounds good, buddy." Dad wrapped his

arm around Parker with a side hug, and they

set off down the canal toward the Bourne

Bridge.

People were fishing along the rocks as they walked down the canal. Kids rode past them on bikes and people were walking dogs with their family. Parker and Dad talked about the summer plans and school in the fall. They walked about a mile until they heard a train whistle.

"Let's walk back! I want to be close when the train crosses!" Parker perked up and spun around. Parker had loved watching the trains on vacation since he was a toddler. The bridge horn sounded, and the

bridge started to drop toward the canal as

the pair started walking back to the truck.

Chapter 4

Emma pushed open the screen door as

Dad and Parker climbed out of the truck.

"Wow, we really beat you this year!" she

yelled with a squinty face.

"Oh darn!" Dad winked at Parker and

tossed his backpack over his back. "Come

on, you two, let's get inside and get unpacked."

Mom was putting away food in the kitchen when they entered the house. "I have ten dollars on the coffee table if anyone wants to go grab some ice cream."

Parker and Emma looked at each other and yelled "YES!" at the same time.

Emma grabbed the money and gave Dad a hug. "I am so happy we are all here, Dad!"

"Me too, kiddo," Dad said with a grin.

"Now go help your brother put the stuff in your room before you guys go get ice cream."

Parker tossed his bags on his bed as Emma appeared. "You ready, sis?"

"Of course I am!" She grabbed his hand and tugged him out the door.

As the pair wandered down the side of the road, they laughed about past trips and their adventures until they finally arrived.

The shop smelled like waffle cones, and

kids were laughing by the big bright

windows.

Emma ordered a small cup of peanut

butter chocolate chip cookie dough. Parker

ordered a waffle cone with strawberry ice

cream. They always ordered the same

things for as many years as they could

remember. "Want to eat outside?" Parker

asked after they paid.

Emma nodded with a mouth full of ice

cream as she pushed open the door and

headed toward the picnic tables. The door

hit a teenage girl as it flung open. "Sorry!"

yelled Emma.

"It's okay." The girl had long red hair

and looked lost. "I wasn't looking where I

was going."

She ran off down the road. Parker

turned to Emma and said "That was weird."

Emma nodded. "But this ice cream is

good!"

Chapter 5

"Oh, I think I see a spot right there!"

Emma said, bouncing in the seat, looking for

a parking space the second they turned off

Route 151.

Mom rolled her eyes as she slowly

drove through one of the small roads in

their favorite shopping spot and turned into the lot behind a make-your-own pottery store. "I think this will do!" she exclaimed as she put the car in park.

Emma climbed out of the car and was leaning on the hood when Mom joined her. "Where to first?"

The duo started walking down a road into a smoothie shop. Mom ordered them each a strawberry banana smoothie as Emma chatted with the owner about how this was one of her favorite stops every

year.

"They don't have any really good

smoothie shops back home. I have been

waiting for this for so long!" Emma shouted

over the blender.

"Well, let me tell you a little secret."

The owner leaned closer onto the counter,

her blue eyes staring right into Emma's.

"Stop by the book store on Common Street.

I think they have a book about how to make

smoothies. You can learn to make some at

home to get you by!"

Mom handed the

smoothie to Emma as she said,

"Ohhh, we just might have to

do that!" She paid for the smoothies, and

they thanked the owner for everything as

they headed out and crossed the street.

"Can we go get a toy for Hunter?"

Emma tugged at Mom's hand and ran into

the most adorable little store for pets.

Emma ran straight to a barrel of squeaky toys. They were shaped like anchors and life vests. "I think these would be perfect, Mom!" she yelled over her shoulder.

"Go ahead and pick one. I am going to grab him a pack of his favorite treats." Mom patted Emma on the head as she walked past her.

Emma started going through the barrel, but a sign hanging in the window caught her eye. The sign read "Lost Dog. Shore Road. 10lbs, wearing a red sweater." In the middle was a picture of the most adorable little white dog. There was small print on the bottom with an email and phone number to contact.

Emma sighed at the thought of how sad she would be if they ever lost Hunter. She quickly grabbed an anchor toy, squeaked it, and met Mom at the cash register.

Chapter 6

"I don't think I am doing this right!"

yelled Parker from the grassy area near the

shore line.

Dad turned around and instantly burst

out laughing. Parker couldn't remember the

last time Dad laughed that loud. "Dude, what happened?"

Parker shrugged with a smile. The fishing rod had somehow fallen to his feet, and fishing line wrapped around his back. He held the cooler in one hand and a bag in the other.

First, let's try putting something down," said Dad with a smile, reaching for the cooler and bag. "Then we will get you untangled and do this the right way."

"But my way is more fun." Parker

laughed. "Or at least funnier."

Dad unwrapped the fishing line and

stood the fishing poles between two rocks.

"That it is." He said as he reached for

Parker's hand. "Now come on down here."

Parker was staring toward a telephone

poll along the path. There was a poster of a

poor little missing dog. "I'd be so sad if

anything happened to Hunter, Dad." Parker

spun toward Dad and almost fell down the

rocks.

"Me too, but I'd be just as sad if I

missed another year fishing because you

hurt yourself again." He laughed. "Now come

on down here, and let's teach you how to

fish!"

Chapter 7

Emma splashed Parker as she ran into the water with a big belly flop. "Hey!" he shouted. She couldn't hear him, though, she was still under water.

The lifeguard's whistles blew, and they all switched spots. Emma's swim teacher,

Mel, walked past and waved to Emma as she came out of the water. "Way to go!" she yelled to her. "Want to do your swim test to the dock today?"

"Oh yeah!" Emma chimed. "After lunch." The lifeguard nodded her head and climbed up onto the lifeguard stand.

"So, tell me about these smoothies..." Parker said to Emma as she returned to his side. "They are for dogs?"

"Yeah! With peanut butter and yogurt

and some other little things." Emma had

stayed up long past Parker reading her

smoothie book last night. "You should come

with us next time we go there. The book

store is so cute."

"You told me ten times already!"

Parker chimed in. "And there is a fountain in

front." He tried to make his voice sound like

Emma's.

She elbowed him hard in the side.

"Don't make fun of me!" she whined.

"Fine!" he teased as he stopped and

looked in a small pool of water.

Emma peaked in too. "What's in here?"

She filled her little red bucket with water

before setting it down next to the pool and

calling Hunter to join them. The giant dog

came running out of the ocean, splashing

Parker.

Parker scooped up a tiny hermit crab.

"Awe. Gotta save you from that big dog jumping in your puddle!" Parker said with a smile as he placed him gently in the bucket.

They stood up and continued their walk, Hunter following behind. They made a few stops along the shore. Emma found some rocks, caught a baby fish, and even found some sea glass. Parker managed to find a few snails and even a clam. By the time they returned back to the lifeguard stand, they had quite the sea collection in their bucket.

"Let me see what you guys found!" Mel yelled down from the lifeguard stand. Emma carefully carried the bucket over to show

her.

"Just a few little critters." Parker said

with a smile.

"Wow!" She exclaimed. "What a good

collection, make sure you let them go

before you head home, though!"

"Of course!" they answered together.

Mel glanced at a poster attached to

the side of the life guard stand. "Wouldn't

want them getting lost from their families

like that puppy."

"Hey! I saw that poster when we were

shopping," Emma said. "Is he from around

here?"

"I saw it at the canal too," Parker

chimed in.

Mel nodded. "His family lives a few

streets away. We have all been keeping an

eye out for him."

"Well, we will too!" Emma announced

strongly.

Chapter 8

"Stop pulling, Hunter!" Emma whined as Dad took the leash from her. "I don't know what's gotten into him today!"

The Millers hiked through the forest toward the water. It was one of their favorite trails, which ended overlooking the bay.

Mom pointed ahead. "Why don't we take a little break at that bench? I think everyone could use some water."

"Sounds good to me," Parker huffed from the back of the pack. He was already pulling his water bottle from his bag when they arrived at the clearing.

"What are you digging at?" Emma walked over to check what Hunter was doing. "Hey, Parker! Come check this out!"

Emma pulled Hunter back as he started

barking.

Parker reached into the brush and

pulled out a dirty red dog sweater. "What is

this?"

"Don't you two know better?" asked

dad as he walked over. "We don't just touch

things we find in the woods."

"It looks like what the puppy was

wearing on those missing dog posters,"

Parker responded, ignoring dad's question.

Emma nodded. "It definitely does, Dad!"

Dad looked at it closer as Hunter

lunged in to sniff it. "Well then, I think we

might have to call that family tonight and

see if they are still missing their puppy."

The kids smiled at each other. "Keep

an eye out while we hike, Emma." Parker

told her as he nudged her in the side.

She giggled. "I always do.

Chapter 9

"Ahhhh!" yelled Emma as peanut butter and banana shot out of the blender. The kitchen was a mess.

Mom turned around with a loud sigh. "Look at this mess. Did you forget to put the cover on the blender again, Emma?"

Hunter came running in and started

licking peanut butter and banana off the

cupboards.

"Well, at least Hunter is happy." Parker

giggled.

They were interrupted by the *DING*

DONG of the doorbell. "I'll get it!" yelled

Dad as he opened the door.

At the front door stood a tall man with

a lost dog poster in his hands. Behind him

was the red headed girl from the ice cream shop.

"Hi. I'm Jack, and this is my daughter Lanna. You called about our dog?" the father said softly.

"Yes! We found this dog sweater while hiking earlier. My kids thought it was the same one in your posters." Dad handed the little red sweater to the girl.

"It's Fluffy's!" The little girl hugged it tight with a frown. "He must be so cold."

Emma popped around the corner with Hunter. "Hi, I'm Emma. I'm sorry your dog is missing. This is Hunter, he's the one who found the sweater."

Lanna smiled and pet Hunter. "Thank you, Hunter. You're a good dog!"

"Dad, do you think, maybe, that Parker, Hunter, and I could help Lanna look for Fluffy?" Emma asked.

Dad crouched down to talk to Emma.

"It's getting late. I don't want to lose you and Parker in the dark."

"But Dad," Emma protested with a whine.

"What about tomorrow after the beach?" Dad said with a smile.

Both girls nodded quickly.

Chapter 10

"Come on, Emma!" Parker ran and

splashed into the water. "Race you to the

dock!"

Emma dove into the water, splashing

Parker on the head. He dove under after

her. Parker banged his hand on the dock as he came up for air.

"You are even clumsy in the ocean," Emma teased.

Parker climbed out of the water and shook out his hair before sitting down on the dock. He didn't like always being clumsy and coming in last. He looked over at Emma and smiled as she jumped into the ocean again.

"Cannonball contest?" he asked when Emma reappeared above water. A cannonball was one of the things Parker could always do better than Emma.

She replied quickly as she climbed back on the dock. "Oh yeah!"

The pair took turns cannonballing for longer than they realized when they found themselves sitting on the dock laughing and catching their breath.

"That was fun." Emma smiled. "Even if you are better at cannonballs than me."

But Parker wasn't listening. He was staring at something near the woods, along the shore.

"Parker!" Emma pushed his arm. "What are you looking at?"

"I... I think I saw something." Parker pointed to a clearing near the trail they walked the day before. "Over there."

Emma squinted to try to see. "I don't see anything, Parker, what did it look like?"

"A white dot." He stood up and walked to the edge. "It ran behind those rocks, I think."

"Do you think it was the missing dog?" Emma joined him on the edge.

Parker looked at his watch. "I'm not sure, but I think it's time we meet up with Lanna and go looking."

Chapter 11

Lanna was sitting in her backyard when Emma and Parker came running up. The siblings were still in their bathing suits and soaking wet. Mom had let them go straight from the dock to Lanna's house.

"Lanna!" Emma yelled. "Parker thinks he saw something!"

Lanna perked up and asked, "When? Where? Was it Fluffy?"

"I'm not sure," Parker mumbled. "We were on the dock, and I saw something white run under some rocks near the woods."

Lanna started lacing up her sneakers. "Ready to go look?"

Emma giggled and looked at her outfit. "I think we need to make a stop so we can get dressed, Lanna."

"Yeah, we aren't going to be much help if we are complaining that we are freezing cold and our legs get scratched up from the woods," Parker responded.

Lanna smiled. "Oh yeah, and we need to get Hunter too."

"I think we will need his nose for this one." Parker smiled.

Lanna grabbed a backpack with a sweatshirt and water bottle and threw it on her back. She told her dad where she was headed, and the trio set off to start their adventure.

They chatted as they walked past the beach and the ice cream shop. When they arrived at Emma and Parker's house, Hunter barked to greet them.

Emma attached Hunter to his leash and tied him up next to the picnic table.

"Lanna, how did you lose Fluffy?" Emma asked quietly.

Lanna looked sad. "I was coming home from the beach, and I had stopped to get ice cream. It was dripping and I was sticky." She frowned.

"You don't have to tell me if you don't want to," Emma interrupted.

Lanna kept going. "I wasn't paying

attention. I opened the back door, and Fluffy

chased a seagull toward the beach."

Emma tried to comfort her new friend.

"I'm sorry. You must miss her a lot."

"I do," responded Lanna, "I hope we

find her soon."

Chapter 12

"Be careful, Emma!" Parker yelled.

"Don't go too far."

Emma was running down the trail with

Lanna. The duo was yelling into the woods

for Fluffy. Hunter's ears were perked up,

and his nose was to the ground.

Parker stopped short at a trail intersection and yelled, "Emma! Lanna! This way!"

The girls came running back. "Are you sure?" asked Lanna. "That trail looks old, like no one's been that way in a long time."

"Yes." Parker nodded. "I'm sure that this trail goes toward the shore. It will bring us to where I think I saw something earlier."

Lanna looked to Emma, and Emma smiled. "If Parker says it's this way, then let's go this way."

The three of them followed Hunter slowly down the trail until Hunter started to pull on the leash.

Parker pulled back. "Calm down, boy."

Hunter barked and pulled harder.

Parker lost his grasp of the leash, and Hunter took off down the path.

"Hunter!" screamed Emma.

The three of them started running

after the dog until they reached the water.

"Fluffy!" yelled Lanna.

Parker turned to Emma and said, "I'm

sorry! We will find him, I promise!"

Emma wasn't listening. "Hunter, come!"

she yelled sternly.

"Shhhhhhhhh," said Lanna.

The Miller kids stopped yelling and

talking. All three listened. "I hear a dog this

way," Lanna started down the shore.

"It's Hunter. I'd know that bark anywhere!" Emma cheered as she ran ahead.

They found Hunter with his nose and head under a rock, barking loudly. Parker grabbed the leash and pulled him out. "Bad dog. Don't run away like that. What are you after?"

Emma reached in her backpack for a flashlight. She sat next to the hole and peered inside. "Umm, Lanna," she whispered,

"come here."

Lanna peaked in the hole. "Fluffy!" she

yelled. A little dirty white ball of fluff

climbed out of the hole and into Lanna's

lap.

"Is it really her?" Parker asked as he

pet Hunter. "Good job, buddy!"

"Yeah, but..." Lanna looked her over.

"She's fat."

Emma's face dropped. "Let's get her

back to your parents. She should see a

vet."

They wrapped Fluffy in a towel and

headed back to the trail.

Chapter 13

Lanna, Emma, and Parker sat quietly in the waiting room at the vet when Lanna's mom and the vet appeared.

"It's okay, kids. Fluffy will be okay."

Lanna jumped up and gave her mom a hug. "Then why was she acting so weird, Mom?" Lanna asked.

"Well, Lanna," started the vet, "I think that sometime next month, Fluffy is going to have some puppies."

Emma gave Parker a giant hug. "Puppies, Parker! Fluffy is having puppies!"

Lanna started laughing. "So that's why she is so fat!"

Everyone started laughing loudly. "Yes, Lanna," her mom answered.

Lanna's mom dropped Parker and Emma off just as the sun was starting to set. "Thank you both for everything."

"We're just happy we could help!" Parker yelled as he shut the door.

"Bye, Lanna!" yelled Emma.

Mom and Dad were waiting on the front steps "Anyone want to join us for a walk down to the beach?"

"Absolutely!" Emma cheered. "I cannot believe this is our last night here."

"I cannot believe that Fluffy is having puppies," Parker said.

"I cannot believe you guys helped find that dog," Dad added.

Mom smiled as they set off toward the beach. "I can believe it all, because I have the most amazing family."

NOTE FROM THE AUTHOR

This story is written about a place that is near and dear to my heart. It is about my home on Cape Cod. Cape Cod is a beautiful beach front location in Massachusetts. The beach area the Miller Family has their vacation home at is called

Monument Beach in the town of Bourne. All

the places and businesses mentioned do

currently exist and are places that I have

visited with my children. The shops in

Mashpee are all real places that I love to

visit with my children.

The Cape Cod Canal has an incredibly

unique bridge called the Train Bridge. This

bridge uses a weight and pulley system to

drop the middle of the bridge to allow the

train to pass over. People spend lots of

time enjoying the bike paths that are on

both sides of the canal and spend time

fishing along the shore.

I encourage you to learn more about

the places in this book. They are all

wonderful and full of the love and

excitement that Emma and Parker feel

during this story.

Made in United States
North Haven, CT
05 May 2022

18911372R00050